For finicky readers

Irving's Delight

"**Lots of fun,** laughs and some excellent satire."
Associated Press

"**An experience in fun.**"
Springfield News and Leader

"**For sheer fun** I would like to recommend *Irving's Delight* ...vintage Buchwald."
The Morristown Record

"**Hilarious** ... *Irving's Delight* will set you rolling on the floor."
KEX Radio, Portland, Oregon

"Art Buchwald is without peer as a satirist."
South Bend Tribune

"**Everyone in the family will enjoy this human, witty, cat-napping mystery.**"
WNYC-FM Radio, New York

Art Buchwald

Irving's Delight

Illustrations by Reynolds Ruffins

AVON
PUBLISHERS OF BARD, CAMELOT, DISCUS, EQUINOX AND FLARE BOOKS

Cover illustration by Bob Guisti originally published by
McCall's Magazine.

AVON BOOKS
A division of
The Hearst Corporation
959 Eighth Avenue
New York, New York 10019

First Avon Printing, September, 1976

AVON TRADEMARK REG. U.S. PAT. OFF. AND
FOREIGN COUNTRIES, REGISTERED TRADEMARK—
MARCA REGISTRADA, HECHO EN CHICAGO, U.S.A.

Printed in the U.S.A.

To Ann, Connie, Jennifer, Joel,
and Little Bits (our cat)

Irving's
Delight

Edgar Allen McGruder burped.

He always burped on Wednesdays—not only just one burp, but ten burps, sometimes twenty, and on a very bad day thirty. Maria Drake, his young, attractive—no, make that beautiful—secretary, always had a bicarbonate of soda with a large glass of water ready for McGruder to take whenever he started to burp. Sometimes it worked; sometimes it didn't.

The reason McGruder always burped on Wednesdays was that it was the day of the week when the Pussyfoot Cat Food Company filmed its TV commercials. Something always went wrong, and just thinking about it would give him gas on the stomach.

McGruder was advertising director of the Pussyfoot Cat Food Company and in charge of spending two million dollars a year to persuade American cat owners to feed their pets nothing but Pussyfoot.

Most of the money went into television, and therefore the commercials for TV had to be perfect. Pussyfoot claimed its cat food contained pure tuna fish as well as vitamins, minerals, and iron (to prevent cats from having tired blood). Pets who were nourished on Pussyfoot would have eyes that sparkled, fur that shone, and they would never, never run away from home.

The truth of the matter was that Pussyfoot was no better or worse than any other cat food. What really made it sell twice as well as Brand X was Irving.

Irving was the star of the Pussyfoot TV commercials. You could call him the Robert Redford of cats—a giant in the pet-food industry and a household word to millions of people in every part of the country.

As cats go, Irving wasn't much to look at. If you saw him in an alley, you wouldn't give him a second glance. Irving was either a white cat with black spots or a black cat with white spots, depending how you liked your cats. He had white whiskers and black cheeks. One ear was white— the other black. His two front paws were white and his two back paws were black. A reporter once wrote that Irving always looked as if some one had thrown an ink bottle at him.

Obviously, Irving's looks were not what made

him a star. What made him such a special cat was that Irving could eat cat food with his paw. People do not know this, but there isn't a cat in a million, ten million, or even a hundred million who will use his paw to scoop out a portion of cat food and put it in his mouth.

How Pussyfoot and Irving got together is an amazing story.

The Pussyfoot Cat Food people were tired of the cats they were using in their commercials. They were also tired of their advertising manager. So they decided to hire the hottest man in the pet TV commercial field. This was Edgar Allen McGruder, who, at twenty-nine years of age, was considered a boy wonder of the business. When he was twenty-five he had taken over the Arf Dog Food advertising, and with one commercial, showing a man eating from the same can of Arf as his dog, McGruder turned the company around.

In order to get him away from Arf, Pussyfoot offered McGruder a fantastic salary, plus shares in the company.

Pussyfoot's approach came at just the right time, as McGruder was getting tired of working with dogs and wanted to go on to something more challenging.

McGruder was a bachelor, a tall, dark-looking

man, full of energy and charm. He was imaginative, intelligent, and straightforward. If he had any faults, only Maria Drake, his secretary, knew them. McGruder was completely absorbed in his work and did not know how to relax. He spent all his waking hours looking for the perfect TV commercial.

When McGruder accepted the Pussyfoot offer, they were thrilled. What he had failed to tell them was that he was allergic to cats. Since childhood, every time he found himself in a room with a cat he got gas on his stomach. One of the reasons he took the job was to see if he could conquer his allergy. So far he had failed.

The first thing McGruder did when he took over the Pussyfoot advertising was to put an ad in all the newspapers announcing that he was holding auditions for a cat to appear in a new television commercial.

The auditions were held in an old movie theater on Broadway. The stage was set up with a large table on which were placed cans of Pussyfoot Cat Food. A television camera was onstage to take pictures of the different cats to see how they looked on the screen.

The morning after the ad appeared, a line of cat owners five block long was waiting to get into the theater. They were holding Siamese cats, Persian cats, Egyptian cats, red cats, black cats, long-haired cats, short-tailed cats, tomcats, and two pet tigers that a lady insisted were legitimate members of the cat family.

McGruder sat as far away from the cats as he

possibly could, in the back row of the theater, watching them on a small television set. Next to him sat Maria, every so often handing him his glass of bicarbonate of soda.

For three days McGruder did nothing but stare at his TV screen and burp.

Despite the great numbers of cats he watched, not one of them looked right for the commercial. By the third afternoon McGruder's eyes were glazed.

About four o'clock a little old lady in tennis shoes walked on the stage with her black-and-white cat. McGruder was so unimpressed with Irving's looks he didn't even bother to glance at the screen. He took that moment to accept a glass of bicarbonate from Maria.

Suddenly he heard one of the assistants shout, "Holy catfish!"

McGruder glanced up. He couldn't believe what he saw on the screen. The cat was eating out of the can with his paw.

He jumped out of his seat and ran down the aisle to the stage. "How did you teach him to do that?"

The little old lady said haughtily, "I did not teach him. Irving has always eaten cat food with his paw."

"I want tape of this," McGruder yelled to the TV cameraman. "Now, Mrs. . . ."

"Miss, thank you. Miss Lila Summersby," the lady said.

Irving ignored all the commotion and just continued dipping his paw into the can and then putting it into his mouth. He never spilled one drop of the cat food. After each swallow, he even licked his paw clean before he went back to the can.

"Great! Fantastic! Unbelievable!" McGruder shouted at the cat. "Irving, I'm going to make a star out of you. You'll be more famous than Paul Newman and Steve McQueen or even Big Bird on Sesame Street. I'll put your name up in lights. Miss Summersby, how much do you want for him?"

Miss Summersby grabbed Irving. "You can't have him. He's not for sale."

"But I need him," McGruder cried. "Don't you understand? Irving is the first animal I've seen who has cat appeal. How about a thousand dollars?"

Miss Summersby started walking off the stage, clutching Irving to her bosom.

"Wait," McGruder said. "If you don't want to sell him, will you rent him to us? We will pay you fifty dollars a week, and all Irving has to do for this is come in every week and eat a can of Pussyfoot Cat Food."

Miss Summersby was still very upset. "I'm not sure Irving wants to do commercials. He doesn't like bright lights."

"Then what on earth did you bring him in here for?" McGruder roared as he tried to stifle a burp.

"Irving and I were just passing by and we saw all these people standing in line holding their cats. We thought it was some kind of cat show and we decided to come in. Then Irving got hungry, and I let him eat one of your cans of food. It was a big treat for him because I can't afford to buy him Pussyfoot. It's much too expensive."

"If you sign a contract with us, we'll give you all the Pussyfoot Cat Food Irving can eat," McGruder pleaded.

"Well," Miss Summersby said, "I'm on social security and it's not easy to feed Irving these days —and myself. If you give us free cat food, does that mean we won't get fifty dollars a week?"

"You'll get both." McGruder assured her.

Irving sat in Miss Summersby's arms, watching what was going on with half-closed eyes. Having finished the can of Pussyfoot, he was

about to take a short nap. Eating always made him very, very sleepy.

Miss Summersby was deep in thought. Finally she said, "I guess there is no harm in it. Besides, it will give us something to do on Wednesdays."

And that's how Irving became the most famous cat in the United States of America.

Once the Irving commercials were put on the air, sales of Pussyfoot Cat Food soared. People were so enchanted with watching Irving eat with his paw that they decided Pussyfoot must be the best cat food of all.

Other pet-food companies were desperate to discover a cat like Irving. But it was impossible.

When McGruder said he was going to make a star out of Irving, he wasn't fooling. Irving's fan mail ran to a thousand letters a week. The Pussyfoot Cat Food Company had to set up a special department to handle all the requests for autographed photographs. They sent back a photo of Irving eating, with a paw print for an autograph.

Children wrote to him. "I love u Irving," one child said. "I dream of u all the time. Pleeze cum to my house I have a nise warm bed." Another letter read, "All of us in the third grade at Public School 35 think you're swell and we

hope our kittens grow up to be just like you. We like it when you lick your paw."

Irving was voted "Cat of the Year," even over Morris the Cat. People paid a dollar just for his poster. The Pussyscat Food Company allowed him to appear at fund-raising events such as Cerebral Palsy and Multiple Sclerosis telethons.

He posed with the "March of Dimes Child" and visited hospitals where children had leukemia.

Everyone loved him.

Most cats exposed to all this heady adulation would have become temperamental and hard to live with.

But not Irving.

Happily, fame did not go to his head. He was still the same gentle, lovable cat he had been before his career in show business. He never got angry when children wanted to pet him. He stuck out his paw when someone wished to shake it, and if a child wanted to kiss him, he licked his or her face.

If a fan wanted his picture, he always stopped to pose for it. Everyone agreed that Irving was a credit to his race.

Because of the success of the Irving commercials McGruder was given a large raise, and although he was the talk of the cat-food business, he still hated Wednesdays.

It seemed that while Irving looked very good on television, he rarely cooperated with the people making the film. One reason was that, since he had all the cat food he wanted, he never seemed very hungry when the Pussyfoot people were ready to shoot the commercial.

McGruder begged Miss Summersby not to feed him on Tuesday, but she wouldn't hear of it.

"Irving would never forgive me," she said.

So every Wednesday in the TV studio, the crew would have to sit around, sometimes for hours, until Irving got hungry. It cost a fortune to pay them all, and McGruder would tear at his hair in frustration. But Miss Summersby, who never appeared to have much to do, didn't seem to mind at all. She just sat there knitting and chatting with the technicians while Irving took a snooze.

This particular Wednesday McGruder had a premonition that something would go wrong again. He didn't know how long his stomach would hold out because of Irving. He was even considering an offer from a birdseed company that wanted him to do commercials with a canary.

At ten o'clock his worst fears came true. Mack, his assistant, came in and said, "Irving hasn't shown up."

Burp.

"I've got the whole crew standing by and we have to have this commercial ready in time for the Super Bowl," Mack said.

McGruder paled. This was the most important commercial of his life. It seems that McGruder's research people had learned that one out of every six persons who watched the Super Bowl either owned a cat or knew someone who did. On the basis of this information he had decided to spend $500,000 to launch a new, secret Pussyfoot Chicken Salad Cat Food during the Super Bowl. Ninety million people would be watching Irving on television at the same time. No pet-food company had ever done anything like it before.

He told Maria to get Miss Summersby on the telephone.

A minute later Maria came back and said, "Her phone doesn't answer."

"Come on," McGruder said. "We'll go to her apartment."

He grabbed his coat and Maria hers.

They dashed out into the street and hailed a cab.

They got in and Maria gave the driver Miss Summersby's address.

It was located on the lower West Side of New York on a dingy street in a very poor neighborhood. When McGruder and Maria got out of the taxi they stared at an old, dark brownstone house.

Maria said, "I didn't know Miss Summersby was so poor."

McGruder was embarrassed and started to feel guilty because the Pussyfoot Company had made so much money from Irving.

"I'm going to raise Irving's salary to a hundred and fifty dollars a week," he said.

They climbed up the steps and rang Miss Summersby's button. There was no reply.

A fat lady with a dust mop came outside and started to shake it in McGruder's face. He began to cough.

"I'm looking for Miss Summersby," McGruder choked.

"She's not here," the fat lady said as she continued to shake the mop.

"Could you tell us where she is?" Maria said.

The fat lady looked at them for the first time.

"It's very important," McGruder said.

"Are you relatives?" the lady wanted to know.

"No," McGruder said. "We're just friends."

The fat lady stood there. "She was taken to the hospital this morning."

"The hospital?" McGruder cried.

"With pneumonia."

"Pneumonia?"

"Yup. The doctor came at six o'clock this morning and then called the ambulance. He said he wasn't sure if she would live."

"Oh, the poor woman." Maria said.

"What about the cat?" McGruder asked. "Where's Irving?"

"The cat's not here."

"You're lying," McGruder yelled. "Where's my Irving?"

"Who are you calling a liar?"

Maria hastily said to the woman, "Don't pay any attention to him. He's just very upset about Miss Summersby. Do you have any idea where Irving might be?"

The fat lady said, "Man came a half hour ago and took the cat away."

"What man?" McGruder yelled.

"I don't know. Some fellow who said he would take care of Irving until Miss Summersby got better."

McGruder held his head in his hands.

Maria said, "Did he give his name?"

"Nope. He acted like he knew Miss Summersby so I didn't ask no questions."

"Did he go in a taxi or an automobile?"

"I didn't notice," the fat lady replied as she became irritated with all the questions.

Maria said gently, "We're sorry to be bothering you but it's very important. What hospital was Miss Summersby taken to?"

The fat lady, who seemed to like Maria, said, "I believe the ambulance said St. Luke's Hospital on it."

"Thank you very much," said Maria, smiling. Then she tugged on McGruder's arm. "We'll go to the hospital."

The fat lady yelled after them. "If you see her, tell her I'll watch after her apartment while she's gone."

Maria and McGruder found another taxi and told the driver to take them to St. Luke's hospital.

27

When they got to the reception desk in the lobby they asked for Miss Summersby's room.

The woman at the desk looked in her card file.

"She's in Room 304, but it says she not allowed to have any visitors."

"Thank you," McGruder said. They walked away from the desk.

"Let's take the elevator," he whispered to Maria.

"But she's not allowed to have visitors," Maria whispered back.

McGruder took Maria's arm and steered her firmly toward the elevator. "Come on and shut up."

At the third floor they got off and walked down the hall to Room 304. There was a large sign on the door. NO VISITORS.

McGruder opened the door. They both looked in.

They couldn't see Miss Summersby. Instead they saw a large oxygen tent over the bed. They could hear heavy breathing.

Just then a doctor came down the hall.

"What are you doing in this room?" he said angrily.

"We've come to see Miss Summersby," McGruder said.

"Can't you read?" the doctor told them. "She is not allowed to have visitors. She is a very sick woman and may die at any moment."

Maria started to cry. McGruder looked sheepish.

"Are you related to Miss Summersby?" the doctor wanted to know.

"No, we're friends of Irving," McGruder said.

"Irving?"

"Her cat."

The doctor stared at McGruder.

"What did you say?"

McGruder spoke fast. "You see, we need Irving for a cat-food commercial, and he's gone."

The doctor was aghast. "Is that why you came up here? To find out where Miss Summersby's cat is?"

"Don't you understand? I need Irving," McGruder cried. "There won't be a Super Bowl if I can't find him."

The doctor looked at Maria. "Is he all right?"

This time Maria took McGruder's arm. "Don't worry, doctor, I'll take care of him. He gets this way about cats all the time."

McGruder said, "Can you tell me when she'll be all right so I can speak to her?"

"I have no idea," the doctor replied. "Miss Summersby must be at least eighty, and I don't

know if she'll be able to pull through this. If Irving means as much to her as he does to you, I would rather that she not know the cat is gone. The shock alone could kill her."

"Thank you, doctor," Maria said.

"Can I ask one more thing?" McGruder said weakly.

"What is it?"

"Do you have any bicarbonate of soda?"

When McGruder and Maria returned to the office they found everyone running around frantically.

"Where have you been?" Mack demanded.

"I've been to see a tennis match at Forest Hills," McGruder replied angrily. "Where do you think I've been? I was looking for Irving."

"Well, where is he?"

"I don't know. He's gone."

"Gone? Oh, boy, are we in for it."

"What do you mean, we're in for it?"

"Mr. and Mrs. Pettibone are down in the TV studio and they're waiting for us to do the commercial."

"You're right," said Maria. "We are in for it."

They went down to the studio. Mr. Rutherford Pettibone was a little red-faced man with a bald head and a white mustache that he must have waxed every night. He had become president of the Pussyfoot Cat Food company through hard work, perseverance, and the fact that he married Zelda Pussyfoot, the only daughter of the company's founder, Hiram Pussyfoot. Zelda was three times as large and one head taller than Rutherford.

She had learned everything about cat food at her father's knee. It was no secret that Zelda Pettibone not only was the power behind Pussyfoot but made all the important decisions as well.

"What's going on around here, McGruder?" Pettibone shrieked.

Zelda Pettibone added, "We've been waiting four hours for you to make this commercial. Do you know how much this is costing the company?"

Pettibone said, "Zelda came all the way down from Connecticut to see this."

"This is a very important day in my life," Zelda said. "When I was cleaning some papers last year I found a note from daddy which I had never seen before. It said, 'Zelda, I have come to the conclusion after sixty years in the cat-food business that we must give cats choices of meals just as we do human beings. I want you to promise me one day that you will develop a cat food with chicken in it and put my name on it.'" Zelda wiped away a tear. "My poor daddy had a dream, and today I am going to see his dream come true. NOW LET'S GET ON WITH THE DAMN COMMERCIAL."

"We can't," said McGruder. "We have no cat."

"No cat?" Zelda screamed. "Where's Irving?"

"He's been stolen or taken away or something. I don't know where he is."

"But what about the Super Bowl?" Pettibone shouted.

"I haven't figured it out yet. I just got the news an hour ago."

"See here," Pettibone said, waving his finger in front of McGruder, "Irving was your responsibility. You should have guarded him night and day. Do you realize we have ten million cans of Pussyfoot Chicken Salad in our warehouses? The future of this company is at stake. The only one who can move those cans is Irving."

"I'm aware of that," McGruder said.

"Young man," Zelda said, "You'd better find that cat and find him fast, or I will see that you never work for another pet-food company in this country again. Poor daddy. He's turning in his grave."

"Please, Zelda, don't get excited," Pettibone said.

"I WANT THAT CAT BACK," Zelda yelled. "AND RIGHT AWAY."

34

"We'll do the best we can," McGruder mumbled.

"NOT THE BEST YOU CAN." Zelda continued her shouting. "I WANT YOU TO FIND HIM. Come, Rutherford. I'm feeling faint."

Pettibone turned to McGruder. "Find Irving if you have to call in the FBI, the Secret Service, and the CIA."

The Pettibones stomped out of the studio.

"Okay, everybody," McGruder said. "We won't be shooting today."

An hour later McGruder's staff was gathered in his office. "Does anyone have any ideas?" he asked.

Mack said, "I think it could have been the work of the Purr-fect Cat Food people. They probably heard we were coming out with chicken salad and decided to sabotage our commercials."

McGruder rejected the idea. "I don't think so. The risks are too dangerous. We could sue them for a million dollars if they had anything to do with it."

"Why don't we offer a five-thousand-dollar reward?" Maria suggested.

"That's the least we'll do. But we don't have much time," McGruder said.

"Can't we train another cat to eat like Irving?" the cameraman suggested.

35

"No way," McGruder said. "The Purr-feet Company has been looking for one for over a year."

"Wait a minute!" Maria snapped her fingers. "I read a story in the *New York Times* yesterday about a famous French detective who specializes in finding lost pets. He was lecturing at the Annual Convention of Missing Animals at the Waldorf Astoria."

"Can you remember his name?" McGruder asked.

"No," Maria said, "but I'll call the *New York Times*. I'm sure they'll be able to tell me where he is."

"Great," said McGruder. "Tell him we'll meet his fee and give him a bonus if he finds Irving."

Maria left the room.

McGruder said, "If we ever find that cat, I'm going to lock him in a safe and only let him out on Wednesdays."

Maria came back fifteen minutes later. "His name is Inspector Alain Pierre Bernheim. He checked out of the Waldorf, but I located him at Kennedy Airport. He is returning to France and said he didn't want to handle the case."

"Oh, no," said McGruder.

"But," Maria smiled, "he's coming back to the city."

"How did you persuade him?"

"I promised I would have dinner with him tonight. He sounds cute."

"I'll be darned," McGruder said.

"But I didn't tell him you were joining us."

"He's coming back because he thinks he's dining with you alone?"

"You know how the French are when they hear a sexy voice. When I said I'd dine with him he said"—and Maria imitated his French accent—" 'There eez always a plane to Paris tomorrow.' Now, where are you taking us?"

"Does it matter?"

"Of course it matters. If you're going to persuade him to take the case, we're going to have to feed him well. What about Les Frères Jacques?"

"That's the most expensive restaurant in New York."

Maria said, "I'm sure Irving would want it that way."

McGruder and Maria and Inspector Alain Pierre Bernheim were just finishing their dessert. Bernheim had ordered snails cooked in garlic, frogs legs cooked in garlic, lamb cooked in garlic, salad with a garlic dressing and—fortunately for both McGruder and Maria—a chocolate soufflé *without* garlic.

Just watching Inspector Bernheim eat made McGruder's stomach feel queasy. He had an omelette, which he could barely get down. Maria had caviar, turtle soup, steak cooked in wine, and a rare French cheese. With the champagne Bernheim had ordered, McGruder figured the check would come to $125.

During the dinner McGruder tried to tell Bernheim all the details of Irving's disappearance. But the French detective did not seem too interested. He was devoting any spare attention he had from eating to Maria.

McGruder studied Inspector Bernheim. He certainly didn't look like the greatest pet detective of all time. He was short, roly-poly, and had red hair and a red beard to match. When he smiled, which he did every time he said something to Maria, you could see a large gold tooth in the front of his lower bridge.

He explained that he had lost his original tooth when he solved the mystery of the disappearance of one of Lord Baskerville's hounds. The hound had a deathly fear of foxes and always ran away when he picked up their scent. Bernheim persuaded Lord Baskerville to surround the outer boundaries of his estate with foxes, thus driving the lost hound straight toward the main house. It worked, but the hound was so frightened he jumped straight at Bernheim, throwing him to the ground and knocking a tooth out of his mouth. Lord Baskerville was so grateful to get the hound back he bought Inspector Bernheim a gold tooth to replace the old one.

The French pet detective was full of stories of his past triumphs. "My greatest case," he told them, "was when I was hired by the Maharajah of Klumpur to retrieve his pet hawk. I chased the hawk through five countries and finally caught up with him in the Himalayas, halfway up Mount Everest, only a few feet from where the

Sherpas say they saw the abominable snowman."

Maria was fascinated. "How did you find him?"

"I knew the hawk ate only a certain kind of rat," Inspector Bernheim said. "This particular breed of rat thrived in only five places. When I failed to find him in Afghanistan, Bhutan, Sikkim, or Tibet, I had no choice but to climb halfway up Mount Everest. I found the hawk sitting on a snow-capped rock eying a small rare mountain goat. I took out the frozen rat I had carefully provided. He dove for it, *zut!* I threw a black hood over the hawk and returned him to the frantic maharajah."

"You must have gotten a large fee for that one," McGruder said nervously.

Inspector Bernheim lit up a cigar. "I charge a thousand dollars a day, plus expenses."

McGruder went white. "For finding pets?"

"Monsieur," the Inspector said, "when someone's pet is involved, money is no object. I once worked for a countess in Sicily. Her husband and her favorite French poodle had been kidnapped by bandits. The countess only hired me to find the poodle."

"And of course you did?" Maria said.

"It was no problem. I gave the bandits five hundred dollars for the poodle, which they gladly accepted. They were asking ninety thousand for the husband. What the brigands didn't know was that the countess would have paid ninety thousand for the poodle, who she was sure loved her, but wouldn't have given five hundred for the count, who she knew didn't."

"Can we get back to Irving?" McGruder said. "Do you think you can find him for us?"

"But of course," said the Inspector. "There is no animal in the world I could not find."

"Where do you think he is?"

"Monsieur, I told Mademoiselle Drake I am not interested in the case."

"Why not?"

"I have to return to Paris to speak at the Sorbonne."

Maria said, "Please, Inspector. Would you do it for me?"

"Mademoiselle, you are making my life difficult."

"A few days," purred Maria, "means nothing to a great man like you, but to us in television, Irving's disappearance could mean we would lose our jobs."

"So"—Bernheim turned to McGruder—"you wish to hire me at my usual rates?"

McGruder gulped. "I guess so. But at a thousand dollars a day you'd better find him fast."

"Très bien," said Inspector Bernheim. "This is a very interesting problem. I haven't worked on a cat case since the Shah of Iran's favorite daughter lost her tabby in an oil well outside of Teheran."

"Please," begged McGruder. "No more stories. Concentrate on Irving. What should we do?"

"We should do nothing."

"Nothing?" said McGruder. "At your prices you want to do nothing?"

"Monsieur McGruder, I have been in New York for only a few days, but even I realize if someone wants to hide a cat in this city, there is no way of finding him. Whoever took the cat has a plan. I am certain in the next few day we will be hearing from the party—or parties—who have Irving in their custody. Now, there is one problem you have not mentioned. Who is the legal owner of Irving?"

"Miss Summersby," Maria said.

"The lady in the hospital?"

"Yes," said McGruder. "Why do you ask?"

"Let us say I find Irving. I have no more legal right to him than the person who is holding him now."

"But he's our cat," McGruder protested. "I made him famous. Everything he is or ever hopes to be he owes to me. His name and Pussyfoot go together like peanut butter and jelly."

"That may be so," Bernheim said, "but I just remember there is something we can all do tonight."

"What is that?" Maria asked.

"We can get on our knees and pray that Miss Summersby gets better."

McGruder scratched his head. "I see what you mean."

"Mademoiselle Drake, may I take you home?" Inspector Bernheim asked.

"I'll take her home," McGruder said.

"Don't I have any say as to who will take me home?" Maria asked.

Both men looked at Maria. She looked back and forth and then said, "I think Inspector Bernheim can take me home."

McGruder was furious. "He should be out looking in garbage pails for Irving."

"We could always go to a movie on Forty-second Street," Maria said.

Inspector Bernheim brightened up. "What would you like to see?"

Maria replied, *Cat on a Hot Tin Roof.*"

"Very funny," McGruder sulked. He called for the check. As he was paying it (with the tip it came to $150) a tall, gaunt man came up to the table.

"Inspector Bernheim," he said. "I thought you were leaving for Paris tonight."

"I beg your pardon."

"Don't you remember me? Russell Baker, pet editor of the *New York Times*."

"Of course, Monsieur Baker. That was a very nice story you did about me in the paper. Unhappily, my plans have changed. Ah, this is Mademoiselle Maria Drake and Monsieur McGruder."

McGruder said, "I know Baker."

"Inspector, what are you doing with people from the Pussyfoot Cat Food Company? Hey, wait a minute," Baker said excitedly. "Nothing has happened to Irving, has it?"

"Of course not," McGruder said quickly." Inspector Bernheim happens to be a friend of Maria's uncle in Paris and we just thought we'd take him to dinner."

"Is that right, Inspector?" Baker asked.

"If he says so," the Inspector replied.

"I'd like to see Irving tomorrow," Baker said suspiciously.

"You can't. He has a cold."

"Monsieur McGruder," Bernheim said, "I believe maybe we should tell Monsieur Baker the truth. If it appears in the *New York Times*, perhaps we may hear from our people sooner than we expected."

"Pettibone will be furious with the publicity," McGruder said.

Baker pulled up a chair, took out his notebook, and said, "Okay, so Irving is missing. Now, what's the rest of it?"

McGruder wearily repeated the story, leaving out all details about the Chicken Salad Cat Food that Pussyfoot was going to launch during the Super Bowl.

"Wow," said Baker. "What a story! They're going to have to make over the front page."

The next morning when McGruder arrived at the Pussyfoot Office Building he found six television trucks parked in front. Reporters and cameras filled the sidewalk.

"Where's Irving?" a reporter demanded.

"Is this a publicity stunt?" a newswoman wanted to know.

McGruder held up his hand. "Ladies and gentlemen, please. I will try to answer your questions. At this moment we don't know where Irving is. His mistress was taken to the hospital and someone, we are not sure who, picked him up. That's all I know."

"Have the police been called in on it?"

"No, but we have hired Inspector Alain Pierre Bernheim, the greatest pet detective of our time, to find him."

"Are you offering a reward for Irving?"

"Yes, we will pay five thousand dollars to anyone who can give us information as to his whereabouts."

"Do you think Irving is still in the country?

"I hope so."

A television reporter asked, "Would you like to make a statement to the people who took Irving?"

McGruder cleared his throat and looked into the camera. 'Yes, I would. Whoever you are, I hope you are taking good care of Irving. He needs a lot of love and a lot of Pussyfoot Cat Food. We will do anything reasonable to get Irving back. Please contact us.

"To the public out there I would just like to say: if you see Irving, please get in touch with us. You all know what he looks like. Do not try to grab him from his unlawful guardians. They may harm him. We will have someone manning the Pussyfoot switchboard twenty-four hours a day. Please, if you have any word, contact us immediately."

"One more question, Mr. McGruder," a TV reporter said. "How do you feel about the loss of Irving?"

A tear came to McGruder's eye. "I feel as if I have lost someone in my own family. . . . Now if you will excuse me."

He pushed through the crowd, opened the door, and went into the elevator.

When he got to his office he found Maria sitting at her desk humming "The Last Time I saw Paris."

"Bonjour, Monsieur McGruder," Maria said.

"Cut that stuff out. Where did you spend my thousand dollars a day last night?"

"We went to Maxwell's Plum. Do you know I have eyes as blue as the Mediterranean, lips as red as a rare Bordeaux wine, skin as smooth as Normandy whipped cream, and a figure that puts the Eiffel Tower to shame?"

"That must have been some evening," McGruder said sarcastically.

"Well, it was better than talking about cat food."

"What did you do after Maxwell's Plum?"

"I don't see as if that's any of your business."

"Bernheim's on my payroll," McGruder retorted.

"If you must know, we went to the Fulton Fish Market and then we saw the sun come up from a Staten Island ferry. Alain said Staten Island reminded him of the Riviera."

"Okay, forget I asked. What's happening?"

"Pettibone is in a rage. He's been calling every

five minutes. He said he wants to see you as soon as you come in."

"Any calls from the catnappers?"

"No." The phone rang and Maria picked it up. "Yes, Mr. Pettibone. He's on his way up."

McGruder left and took an elevator up to Pettibone's office.

The secretary indicated he could go in. He opened the door. Pettibone was sitting behind his desk and Zelda Pettibone was towering over him. The front page of the *New York Times* was on his desk.

"Well," said Pettibone. "To coin a new phrase, you really let the cat out of the bag."

"I'm sorry about that," McGruder said.

"Do you know what's happened since this story appeared?" Zelda Pettibone said.

"No."

"The stock of Pussyfoot Cat Food has dropped six points," Zelda said. "The bank called up this morning and said because we no longer have Irving they were going to call in our loan—the money we borrowed to produce ten million cans of Chicken Salad Cat Food."

"But Bernheim thought the publicity would be a good idea," McGruder said.

"Who is Bernheim?"

"Inspector Bernheim, the greatest retriever of lost animals in the world. He has a gold tooth in front of his mouth to prove it."

"And what does he have to do with us?"

"I've hired him to find Irving."

"A Frenchman?" Zelda said in dismay.

"He speaks good English," McGruder assured her. "Look, you told me to get Irving back. If anyone can find him, Bernheim can. He's unbelievable. He once found Prince Charles's gerbil when it escaped from its cage in Buckingham Palace. The queen would have knighted him if he had been a British citizen."

"How much are we paying this inspector?" Pettibone asked.

McGruder hesitated. "One thousand dollars a day."

Both Pettibones looked as if they were going to faint. "You did this without consulting us?"

"I had to. He was going back to France last night. There is nobody in America like him. Believe me, if he finds Irving it will be a bargain."

"How much time do we have?"

"Three days. The commercial has to be at the network twenty-four hours before the Super Bowl."

"Can't they postpone the Super Bowl?" Zelda asked.

"I'm not sure," said McGruder, "but I'll ask them."

"Get out of here," Pettibone said. "And I want to be kept informed as to what is going on."

Zelda said, "And the next time you hire a Frenchman for a thousand dollars a day, you'd better ask permission first."

"Do not despair. I'm sure Bernheim will find our cat," McGruder said.

He returned to his own floor. "What news?" he said to Maria.

"The switchboard is jammed with people who swear they've seen Irving."

"Tell the operators to take everyone's name. We may get lucky."

"The art department is printing three thousand posters of Irving to be distributed all over the city with the offer of the five-thousand-dollar reward."

"Good."

"The network called. They said if you're not going to use your time on the Super Bowl, the Tang orange drink company would like it."

"Tell them we're going to use it, and not to sell it to anyone."

"Oh, and Alain called."

"Alain?"

"Inspector Bernheim. He wants us to join him

for lunch at La Plume de Ma Tante. He says it was recommended by his cousin."

"Good gravy. Can't the man talk without eating?" McGruder said.

"I've never been to La Plume de Ma Tante," Maria said. "I hear it's even more expensive than Les Frèrees Jacques."

"And you're not going, either. I can't afford to feed you and Inspector Bernheim. Besides, you have to answer the phone."

"Thanks, big spender," Maria said. "Suppose Alain pays for me?"

McGruder pointed. "The phone."

At one o'clock McGruder walked over to La Plume de Ma Tante. Bernheim was standing at the bar with a crowd around him. "Ah, Monsieur McGruder, I was just telling these nice people about the time the Prince of Monaco lost his favorite elephant. It was a very baffling case because it's impossible to hide an elephant in the tiny principalité of Monaco. I searched and searched. Finally I looked out into the port and I noticed a large three-masted sailing yacht owned by a Greek shipping millionaire. What attracted my attention was that it kept listing to starboard despite the fact there was no wind. I brought the prince's female elephant down to the port and hit her hard on the derrière. She let out an angry cry. From the bottom of the yacht came the answering cry of a male elephant.

"When we confronted the Greek shipping king he denied he knew there was an elephant on board his boat. The truth was he was taking it back to his private zoo. The prince was so angry he banned the Greek shipper from Monaco for life."

McGruder said, "Come on, let's get a table." When they sat down McGruder said, "What did you find out about Irving?"

"Please, Monsieur McGruder, not before we eat. I think today I shall have clams with garlic, trout with garlic, and crème caramel, all with a nice light white wine."

McGruder looked at the prices and ordered cream of chicken soup and a green salad.

After the clams arrived Berheim said, "I've had a very interesting morning. I have been visiting New Jersey."

"What the heck for?"

"I went to Paterson, New Jersey. Do you know Paterson?"

"I've heard of it, but I've never been there."

"Paterson is the birth place of Miss Summersby."

"So?" McGruder said impatiently.

"Did you know Miss Summersby had a sister?"

"No, I didn't. Where is she?"

"She's dead," said Bernheim, sopping up the sauce from his clams.

"You spent all morning in New Jersey to find out Miss Summersby's sister was dead?"

"Ahah. I also found out another bit of information. Miss Summersby's sister, a Mrs. Wicker, had a son named Oren.

"Oren, how do you say? was the black sheep of the family. The neighbors remember he used to kill birds with a BB gun."

"Go on."

"He owned a dog which he beat every time he walked him."

Bernheim sipped his wine. "It's not a very good year."

McGruder was ready to scream with impatience.

"But the animals he hated the most were cats."

"Why?"

"At first, when he was small, because they used to steal the birds he shot with his BB gun. Then because his aunt loved cats. Oren Wicker always made nasty remarks about his aunt's pets behind her back. But when he saw her, he pretended he liked them. He was her only relative."

"Do you think Oren stole Irving?"

"It's a possibility," Bernheim said, cutting into his trout. "No one knew Miss Summersby had been taken to the hospital except the landlady. A few hours later a man showed up and took the cat. Oren Wicker would have to be considered a strong suspect."

Suddenly Maria appeared in the dining room.

Bernheim's face brightened up. He tried to kiss her hand but there was an envelope in it.

Maria said, "A little boy said a man gave him a quarter to deliver this to us."

She handed it to McGruder. "I opened it up."

McGruder read it. WE HAVE IRVING. IF YOU EVER WANT TO SEE HIM ALIVE AGAIN YOU WILL HAVE TO PAY US $100,000. DO NOT GO TO THE POLICE OR THE FBI—AND GET THAT FRENCHMAN OFF THE CASE OR WE'LL KILL THE CAT.

Bernheim examined the letter. "Hand printed. It sounds serious."

"What are we going to do?" McGruder said.

Bernheim poured a glass of wine for Maria. "To last night."

"Will you two knock it off and get down to business?" McGruder screamed.

"We must proceed carefully," the Inspector said. "First, we do not know if the man who sent this letter really has the cat. I remember once in Ireland a man named McGarry paid two hundred thousand dollars' ransom for his pet beagle. After he paid it he discovered someone else had stolen the dog and only wanted twenty-five thousand dollars. Had I gotten into the case in time I could have saved McGarry a hundred and seventy-five thousand dollars."

Maria said, "How can we find out if they really have Irving?"

"They will be contacting you again. You must demand proof. They must send you some of Irving's fur. Tell them you want to compare it."

"But," McGruder protested, "we don't have any fur to compare it with."

"They don't know that."

"What will you do?" McGruder asked.

"I will go back to Paris."

"You can't go back to Paris."

"I will not go back to Paris, but we will announce I am going back to Paris. I will hold a press conference at Kennedy Airport saying I am returning to France because I can't drink the American water. Then I will get on the front end of the plane and leave by the rear. Our catnappers will believe I no longer have anything to do with the case."

"I like it," McGruder said.

"Now," Maria said, "I see why you charge such high fees."

"From there on I will go, how do you say?— under the covers. I shall stay at a motel under the name of Bob Gross, a good American friend of mind. We shall only meet when we have something to discuss."

"You mean you won't be eating in these expensive French restaurants anymore?" McGruder brightened up.

"Alas, when I go under the covers, my stomach goes with me. Now return to your office and tell the press I have given up on Irving and am going back to France on the six o'clock PanAm flight. Then stay in your office. I would not be surprised if you hear from our friends again—very soon. Maria, why don't you help me pack?"

McGruder growled. "I need her back at the office."

"C'est la vie," Bernheim shrugged.

"What did he say?" McGruder asked Maria.

"He said he would climb Mount Everest for me."

McGruder counted out sixty-three dollars to pay for the lunch.

McGruder and Maria returned to the office. They weren't prepared for what was waiting for them. In the lobby and all up and down the halls of the Pussyfoot Cat Food Company were cat owners holding their pets.

The receptionist was hysterical. "Oh, Mr. Mc-Gruder, what are we going to do with all these cats?"

"What's going on?"

"They're all pet owners who read that Irving is gone and they hope one of their cats can replace him."

Several of the owners were listening. They decided McGruder was the man they were waiting for.

One lady said, "My cat eats nothing but Pussyfoot." She took out an open can of Pussyfoot, placed it on the carpet and said, "Matilda, show the nice man how you eat."

Matilda stuck her nose in the can and started to eat, just like any cat would.

McGruder shook his head. "I'm sorry."

A man and woman with a large white cat in her arms blocked McGruder's path. "Caroline can say Pussyfoot."

The man said, "Say Pussyfoot, Caroline."

Caroline looked from one to the other and yawned.

"Please, darling Caroline," the lady said. "Speak for the nice man. Say the magic word."

The man pulled Caroline's tail and Caroline went:

"Meoowww!"

"There," said the man. "What did I tell you?"

McGruder said, "Tell me what?"

"Did you hear her say Pussyfoot? That's the only word she knows," the woman said.

McGruder turned to Maria. "I think I'm going nuts."

Maria tried to keep a straight face.

"Watch this," a young man said in front of McGruder's office door. He put his cat down. "Simon, what do you think of Pussyfoot Cat Food?"

Simon did a somersault.

McGruder said, "Simon, what do you think of Purr-fect Cat Food?"

Simon did another somersault.

"He seems to flip for everything."

"You stupid cat," the man shouted at Simon.

McGruder turned to the crowd of clamoring people holding their cats up.

"Ladies and gentlemen, thank you for coming. We are very optimistic that we will find Irving, and at the moment we are not looking for a replacement. If at some future date Irving is not found, we will be in contact with all of you. Now, for the safety of all your beautiful pets, will you kindly leave the building?"

McGruder ducked into his office with Maria. The phone was buzzing. The operator said, "It's Dr. Parker at St. Luke's Hospital."

McGruder picked up the phone. "Yes, doctor?"

"Now you've done it," Dr. Parker said. "Miss Summersby is in shock."

"Shock?"

"She heard over the radio in her room that Irving had disappeared and she seems to have lost her will to live. I warned you if word got out she wouldn't be able to take it."

"I'm sorry, doctor, but I didn't think she would hear about it in her hospital room. When we saw her she was sealed off from everything."

"Not the radio. You've done a terrible thing, Mr. McGruder—a terrible thing."

"I feel awful about this. What can I do?"

"Find Miss Summersby's cat."

McGruder hung up. He told Maria what the doctor had said.

"Before, all we had to worry about was a Super Bowl commercial, now we have a person's life at stake."

The phone buzzed again. The operator said, "There's a man on the phone who refuses to give his name."

McGruder signaled to Maria to pick up the extension and write everything down.

The man said, "Did you get our note?"

"Yes, I did."

"Did you fire the Frenchman?"

"Yes, he's leaving tonight for France."

"How do we know that?"

"Watch the eleven o'clock news tonight."

"What about the police?"

"They're staying out of it at our request."

"You better be telling the truth or we're slitting Irving's throat."

"How do we know you have Irving?"

"He's sitting right here eating some of your stinking cat food."

"I want a sample of his fur to make sure he's our cat."

"That's just a stall. All right, you want to

know if we have Irving. You've been working with him for a year, right?"

"Yes."

"Okay. Irving has a black mole the size of a quarter behind his left ear."

"You're right. No one would know that. But how do I know he's still alive?"

"That's the chance you're going to have to take. Now this is what we want you to do. There is a cemetery in Fairview, Long Island. It's called the Heavenly Rest Home for Pets. You're to come out to the cemtery at ten o'clock tomorrow night—alone. Bring a hundred thousand dollars in hundred-dollar bills. They are to be in a paper bag. Walk down the center lane of the cemetery until you get to the last row against the fence. Turn left, and stop at the third tombstone, which has inscribed on it 'Good-bye Cokey—My Best Friend—June 12, 1963—October 30, 1974.' Drop the bag in front of it and do not look around. Someone will always be watching you. Return the way you came. At the gate-house will be Irving in a canvas bag. If you don't follow these instructions to the letter, one of my people will stick a knife into the bag, and then you can dig a grave for Irving in the cemetery. Tomorrow night at ten—and no tricks."

He hung up.

"Get me Bernheim," McGruder said.

Maria dialed the Waldorf and asked for him. She told McGruder:

"They say he's checked out. I think I better notify the press he's leaving tonight for France."

"Yeah, do that."

As Maria left the office Mr. and Mrs. Pettibone marched in.

"What news?"

"They're holding Irving for ransom," McGruder said.

"We'll pay it. How much do they want?"

McGruder looked at both of them. "One hundred thousand dollars."

"We won't pay it," Pettibone said.

Zelda Pettibone said, "And what about my daddy's chicken salad?"

"Zelda," Pettibone said, "no cat is worth a hundred thousand dollars."

"If my daddy was alive," Zelda said, "he would say, 'Damn the expense; the cats come first.'"

"Your father sounds like he was a wonderful man," McGruder told her.

"The Pussyfoots always had courage," Zelda said.

"Well," said her husband, "if it means that much to you, we'll pay it. But I want the serial numbers on every one of those bills. I'll call the bank and tell them to get the package ready. I want that money back, McGruder."

"First Irving, then the money," McGruder said.

"Why don't we call in the FBI?" Pettibone demanded.

"We'd be signing Irving's death warrant. I talked to one of his captors. He's a vicious man."

"Do you have any idea who they are?" Zelda asked.

"Bernheim is following up some leads. By the way, if you're watching the news tonight, you're going to see Bernheim say good-bye to America. Don't pay any attention to it. He's just throwing off the catnappers."

Pettibone said, "This whole business is getting out of hand. I'm not sure it's all worth it."

Zelda said coldly, "No one asked you."

Pettibone said meekly, "Right, keep up the good work, McGruder. Anything is worth finding Irving."

Zelda said, "Did you ask the Super Bowl people if they would postpone the game?"

"Yes, I did," McGruder replied wearily, "but unfortunately it was too late. The teams have their hearts set on playing on Sunday."

Mr. and Mrs. Pettibone walked out and Maria came in.

"Alain just called."

"What did he say?"

"He asked me to have tea with him at the Plaza just before he goes under the covers."

McGruder groaned.

"He also said he wants us to meet him at his motel tonight. And he told me if they called again to keep them on the phone as long as possible and try to trace the call. He said to tell them it will take a few days to get the ransom together."

It won't work. They're too smart. I'd better go to the bank and pick up the hundred thousand."

"You're not going to walk around with a hundred thousand?"

"No, I'll hide it somewhere. I've got it. I'll put it in one of the TV cameras in the studio. No one will find it there."

"I must say," Maria said, "this is a lot more fun than the advertising business."

"You stay here."

"No tea with Alain?"

"No tea with Alain," McGruder said and walked out.

Since so many newspaper men were standing in front of the building, McGruder took the elevator to the basement and then walked out the garage entrance. He made sure he wasn't being followed. The bank had been alerted to the fact that he was coming and he was ushered into a vice-president's office. Five tellers were seated at a table making records of the numbers on the one-hundred-dollar bills. They were the bank's most trusted employees because if word were to get out that McGruder had picked up the ransom money, Irving's goose was cooked.

Finally the vice-president handed McGruder the package.

"Do you want to count it yourself?" he asked him.

"No, thanks. It would take me a week. I'll have to take your word for it."

He signed a receipt for the money.

"Here's a shopping bag," the vice-president of the bank said. "Put the money in that. No one would suspect you were carrying a hundred thousand dollars."

When McGruder got back to the building, Russell Baker of the *New York Times* spotted him as he tried to go into the garage.

"McGruder," said Baker, "you owe me a favor. Give me something for tomorrow's paper."

"I don't have anything to give you," McGruder said. "We haven't heard a thing since last night."

"Where's Bernheim?"

"He's off the case."

"Off the case? That's a story. Why did you fire him?"

"I didn't say we fired him. Let's say we reached a mutual agreement that he wasn't the right person. After all, he doesn't know New York, he has no contact with any of the known pet underworld, and he was too damn expensive."

Baker was writing in his notebook. "Have you hired anyone to take his place?"

"We're interviewing other detectives now."

"But nobody is better than Bernheim," Baker said.

"Maybe in France, but the Pussyfoot Cat Food

Company believes when it comes to law enforcement, the American police are the best."

"What have you got in the shopping bag?"

"Groceries for my poor sick mother. Now I have to go."

McGruder ducked into the garage and took the elevator to the studio floor. No one was there. He found a screwdriver and unscrewed the back plate of the television camera and took out the insides, which came as a unit. He put the wires and tubes in a closet and then stashed the money in the empty TV camera. He rescrewed the plate. And as he did so, McGruder smiled. He was pleased with his hiding place.

Then he went down to his office. It was seven o'clock and no one was there. He sat in his chair and flicked a button which turned on the television set he kept in his office so he could watch the Pussyfoot commercials.

Walter Cronkite came on the screen. "A nationwide search continued today for Irving, America's favorite cat, believed to have been kidnapped this morning from his home in New York City.

"Irving's whereabouts have been reported as far away as Seattle, Washington. One rumor circulating this morning was that Irving was being held hostage by a fanatical band of animal lovers who were demanding the release of every animal in the Bronx Zoo. Another story, which was later denied, said that Irving was being held in the Soviet Embassy in Washington where his abductors had sought asylum. Still another story making the rounds is that Irving had been spirited out of the United States and had been taken to Cuba. All these stories, I repeat, are just rumors. At this moment there is no hard news as to where Irving is or if he is even alive.

"Reaction to Irving's disappearance has been coming in from all over. The President, through his press secretary, said that he, his wife, and his whole family were praying for Irving's safety. Henry Kissinger offered to postpone a trip to China to negotiate with the kidnappers if they were willing to meet with him. The Purr-fect Cat Food Company has added another five thousand dollars to the reward of five thousand offered by the Pussyfoot Cat Food Company. Purr-fect President Sam Grinsley said, 'It is our way of showing solidarity for our friends over this outrageous crime.'

"And now we take you to Kennedy Airport where Inspector Alain Pierre Bernheim, the world's greatest pet detective, is holding a live press conference before he returns to Paris."

The screen showed a woman. "This is Connie

Chung at Kennedy Airport where Inspector Bernheim is about to leave for France."

McGruder saw Bernheim struggling with his luggage.

"Inspector Bernheim, why at this moment are you returning to France?"

"Because the American water makes me sick, I hate the New York traffic, I can't sleep since the garbage trucks go bang-bang at five in the morning, and the Pussyfoot Cat Food Company won't pay my fee."

"You mean you're stepping out of the case over a fee?"

"Young lady, I earn my living finding pets. I do not ask people to work for them. They hire me. The Pussyfoot Cat Food people with all their millions thought my price was too high. So au revoir."

"But this more than just a lost cat, this is Irving."

"That is not my affair. To me, Irving is just an animal. I stayed at the request of Mr. McGruder. But when I found out that the Pussycat Company was so cheap, I became homesick for Paris."

McGruder's phone rang.

"Are you watching Cronkite?" Mr. Pettibone yelled.

"Yup, he's putting on a good act."

"Good act? He's telling the entire country we're cheap."

"Yeah, you have a point. Well, there's no sense crying over spilled milk." McGruder hung up.

Walter Cronkite came back on. "And now let's go to Eric Severeid and hear his thoughts on Irving."

Severeid came on the screen. "This country has withstood some terrible shocks in the last fifteen years, but the loss of a cat is something we can all identify with. This question is, are we now entering a period where it is not even safe for a dog or a cat to walk down the street alone? Has this civilization weakened to the point where a helpless cat must fear for his safety? Law and order has taken its toll of our civil liberties. Will Irving's death, if he is dead, agitate pet vigilantes to take the law into their own hands? Irving symbolizes the last hope of a new era for this country. With him we are everything—without him we are nothing. Let us wish that whoever has Irving realizes the potential for good or evil he holds in his hands. We are now at the precipice. Irving's demise would push us over into a watershed from which no freedom-loving people can ever hope to recover."

McGruder's phone rang again.

"What did Severeid mean?" Pettibone wanted to know.

"Beats me," McGruder said.

Cronkite came back on the screen. "Before signing off, I speak for millions of people who say, 'God bless you, Irving.' . . . And that's the way it is January eighteenth. This is Walter Cronkite . . . Good night."

Inspector Alain Pierre Bernheim, alias Bob Gross, was eating a hamburger when McGruder and Maria came to his motel room at nine o'clock at night.

"This is the worst case I've ever worked on," he said.

"Why do you say that?" McGruder asked him.

"Because this is the worst meal I've ever eaten."

"I saw the press conference," McGruder said.

"I thought it was very convincing." Bernheim replied.

"You certainly were. Pettibone had a fit. Why did you have to call us cheap?"

"I decided our cat-stealing friends had to be convinced, and what better reason for getting off the case than someone will not pay you your fee."

"I watched you on the Chancellor show, Alain." Maria said. "You were brilliant."

"He's brilliant and we're cheap," McGruder said.

Bernheim wiped his hands on a paper napkin.

"They sent the hamburger on a plastic plate with a plastic knife and plastic spoon, and my coffee came in a plastic cup. Even the tomato on the hamburger was plastic."

"Can we talk about the case?" McGruder asked.

"All right. Did they call back after giving you your instructions?"

"No. We stayed at the office until we came over here."

"Let me see the dialogue again between you and the man."

Maria handed him several sheets of paper, and Bernheim studied them. "Do you know about this Heavenly Rest Home for Pets?"

"No," said McGruder. "Fairview is quite far out on the Island. It's at least a two-hour drive from the city."

"Why don't we go out there?"

"Tonight?" Maria said.

"Why not? They are expecting us tomorrow night. I want to see this place. They could be watching tomorrow in the daytime."

"Okay," McGruder sighed.

"Let us stop by a drugstore and buy a flash-light," Bernheim said.

A half hour later they were on the expressway. McGruder drove, Maria sat in the middle, and Bernheim on the outside.

The Inspector started talking about cats. "The cat has been all things to all men. The Egyptians worshipped it as a god; later on in Europe it was considered a witch. France used to burn cats as a sacrifice until King Louis the Third put a stop to it.

"Superstition dies hard in France, and to this day in the countryside people have strong beliefs about the power of cats.

"Some peasants say that if you kill a cat you will die a horrible death."

"I wish we could get that message to the cat-nappers," McGruder said.

"In your country a black cat is an omen of bad luck. In our country it is just the opposite. In Brittany they believe a black cat can bring you a fortune overnight. In France it is said that if a maiden takes very good care of her cat she will find herself a handsome husband. In the north of the country if a girl refuses to marry a man they say she has 'given him the cat.'

"We also believe that the cat is associated with female, and women were made from the tail of a cat and therefore are more malicious than men."

"So much for women's lib," Maria said.

"But they were extremely intelligent and sensitive creature with a sixth sense. And very loyal. I have seen them sit on the bed of a sick person for weeks, even months, and refuse to move because they think their owner is going to die.

"But alas," Bernheim concluded, "I do not want to depress you. This Long Island is very long, isn't it?"

"I'll say this for those pigs," McGruder said. "They didn't want to make it easy for us to get Irving back."

When they arrived at the cemetery it was pitch black. Bernheim took out the flashlight and the three approached the entrance. There was no one in the gatekeeper's house and the gate was locked. They walked along the outside wall.

"We will have to climb over," Bernheim said. He gave the flashlight to Maria and made a step with his hand so McGruder could get over. Then he lifted Maria. He seemed to be having more difficulty with Maria than the wall warranted, and McGruder found himself getting very angry.

When she finally got over, McGruder whispered, "You sure took a long time getting over the wall."

She whispered back, "Alain couldn't find the right part of me to lift over."

"I don't like what's going on between the two of you."

"Well," retorted Maria, "maybe he thinks of me as being more than just a secretary."

By this time Bernheim had joined them. The cemetery was eerily quiet. Bernheim flashed his light at a tombstone. WE LOVED YOU CHARLEY——REST IN PEACE.

He flashed to another stone. TOMMY—DEAREST OF ALL PARROTS—MAY YOU NEVER USE FOUL WORDS IN HEAVEN.

"This is quite a place," Maria said.

McGruder pointed. "There's the path I was supposed to take."

They walked on the pebbles and their footsteps echoed throughout the cemetery.

As they neared the last row a bearded old man suddenly jumped up in front of them!

Maria screamed.

McGruder and Bernheim jumped back.

"Get out of my cemetery," the man shouted, waving his hands.

"Your cemetery?"

"At night it's my cemetery. I'm the only one permitted in here."

"Are you the night watchman?"

"No, but I come here every night to talk to Seth."

Bernheim flashed the light on a tombstone. SETH—MAY YOUR BARKING KEEP THE ANGELS AWAKE. OCTOBER 18, 1973.

"Seth," said the old man, "was my Irish setter. I used to talk to him all the time. My wife is gone so I have no one to talk to anymore. I come every night and we have some good chats. But lately this place is worse than Grand Central Station."

"Have there been other people here?" Bernheim asked.

"There certainly have been. Last night there were two men over there shining their light around and messing with the tombstone."

"In the last row by the fence?" McGruder asked.

"Yup, they were arguing and fussing about something."

"Can you remember what the argument was about?"

"I don't know. It had something to do with a cat."

"What exactly did they say?" Bernheim asked.

"I can't remember."

"It's very important," McGruder said.

The old man said. "Well, I think they said something about hiding in that grave digger's tool shed over there. One fellow said they should kill the cat and the other was arguing the cat should live."

"Did they see you?" McGruder asked.

"No, I hid. I thought they were police and were going to kick me out of the cemetery. I'm not supposed to be here after dark."

"Did they say anything else?"

"That's all I can recall."

"What did they do then?" Bernheim asked.

"They left. Oh, yeah, one of the fellows—I think he was the one who didn't want to kill the cat—did a real mean thing. He took fresh flowers off of someone's grave and placed them on the grave they was standing in front of."

Bernheim walked over to the tombstone where the flowers were and shone the light. It said: COKEY.

He returned to the group. "Where does the caretaker live?"

"Waldo?"

"Yes, Waldo."

"Down the road in a yellow house by the stop sign. 'Waldo Cummings' it says on the mailbox."

"Thank you very much," said Bernheim. "You've been most kind."

"Grand Central Station," the old man muttered. "Seth, they won't let you sleep."

"Good night," Bernheim said as he started walking down the path out of the cemetery.

"Don't you want to look around?" McGruder asked.

"I don't think that is necessary. Our next job is to find out who owned Cokey."

Waldo Cummings was not very thrilled at being awakened at one o'clock in the morning. McGruder apologized by placing a twenty-dollar bill in his hand.

Waldo accepted the apology and let them in his house.

Did he know who owned Cokey?

He got out his tombstone record book. A family named Springbrook.

Had he ever seen any members of the Springbrook family at the cemetery?

The son, Carl Springbrook, came out every once in a while.

Did he have an address for the Springbrooks?

Waldo looked in another ledger. 555 Chowderbox Lane, Southampton.

Bernheim wrote this all down. "Thank you. It's possible we may have to call on you again."

"It will cost you more than twenty dollars,"

Waldo said. "If you wake me out of my sleep."

Bernheim told McGruder to head to Southampton.

"Why are you so sure the owner of Cokey is one of our catnappers?" Maria asked.

Bernheim replied. "A man does not take flowers off a grave and put them on another grave unless he has a sentimental attachment for whoever is buried underneath."

"That's brilliant, Alain," Maria said.

"It doesn't take a thousand dollars a day to figure that out." McGruder grumbled. "Why can't we go home tonight and get some sleep?"

"Because, Monsieur McGruder, I am afraid we are working, how do you say, against the clock. Irving's life is in serious peril."

"Why?" Maria asked.

"The report of the argument in the graveyard disturbs me. When two men are having an argument and one wants to kill an animal and the other doesn't, usually the one for murder is more dominant and he wins. We know Miss Summersby's nephew, Oren, has a serious record of hurting animals. Carl, on the other hand, cared enough about his pet to steal flowers for him. I am afraid if we don't get to Irving soon, Oren will decide the argument."

McGruder speeded up the car. They arrived at

Chowderbox Lane. A large hedge protected the house, which was hidden from the road. The driveway twisted and turned for a quarter of a mile.

"Why would someone who lived in a house like this want to steal a cat?" Maria said.

"I hope we got the right place," McGruder said.

At last they arrived at the house, a large colonial mansion with six white columns. There were no lights on.

They approached the door and Bernheim rang the bell.

They waited. Finally a light went on in the basement. They waited some more. Then they heard footsteps. The door, which had a chain on it, opened an inch.

A frightened eye peered out.

"Madame Springbrook?"

"Nobody home. Nobody home," the voice said in an accent.

Inspector Bernheim started to speak French. The voice responded in French. They went back and forth. The woman finally unlatched the chain and let them in. She was in a housecoat.

Bernheim kissed her hand.

"Is she French?" Maria asked.

"Belgian," Bernheim said. "She's the Springbrooks' housekeeper. The Springbrooks are in Florida."

"Carl, too?" McGruder asked.

Bernheim spoke to the lady in French again. She replied, furiously waiving her hands in anger.

Bernheim translated. "Carl is living over the garage with another man. The Springbrooks kicked Carl out six months ago and told him never to come back. But he returned as soon as they left."

"Ask her if she's seen a cat?" McGruder said.

Bernheim repeated the question in French.

"She hasn't seen one, but she's heard one, screaming as if it was being tortured."

"We'd better call the police."

They heard a cat shrieking as if in pain.

Bernheim said, "We don't have time. Where's the garage?" he asked the housekeeper.

"Over there." She pointed away from the house.

McGruder said, "You stay here, Maria."

He and Bernheim went running down the path toward the garage, which was a separate building three hundred yards from the house.

It was dark, but there was a car parked in front of it. Bernheim took the air out its tires. He studied the building. "The apartment is up there. The stairway is on the side of the garage. It seems to be the only door. Let us go up."

"But we don't have any weapons or anything."

"Courage, Monsieur McGruder. Surprise is better than weapons."

They went to the door and opened it softly.

Bernheim led the way up the stairs.

Bernheim gently opened the door to the apartment. He switched on the light.

Two men sat up in their beds, startled. The room was a mess, with clothes all over the floor, empty beer cans, and dirty plates on the furniture.

"What the heck?" one of the men said.

"What do you want?" the other man said.

"We want the cat." McGruder told them.

"We don't have any cat."

"Do not play games with us, messieurs."

"It's the lousy Frenchman," one man said. "I told you, Carl, they would double-cross us."

"So", said Bernheim, "you are the famous Oren."

Oren got out of his bed in his underwear. "We don't know nothing about a cat. Now get out of our apartment."

Carl, the other man, said, "We have no cat. Search around if you want to."

McGruder went to the closet and pulled it open. Bernheim looked under the beds. They went into the bathroom—no cat.

Oren and Carl were smiling. "We told you there was no cat."

Both McGruder and Bernheim were puzzled.

"I have a good mind to call the police," Carl said, "and arrest you for breaking into my apartment."

Oren said, "Get out."

Bernheim said, "I guess we'd better go."

McGruder turned to leave, and then he started burping.

"What's the matter?" Bernheim asked him.

"There's a cat somewhere around here or I wouldn't be burping."

McGruder walked across the room. He looked up at the ceiling."

"Look, Inspector, there's a trap door up there."

"Alors," said Bernheim. He pushed a bed under the trap door and climbed on it. Oren knocked him off the bed. McGruder jumped for Oren and Carl hit McGruder from behind. Both Bernheim and McGruder went sprawling.

Oren had climbed up on the bed, opened the trap door and pulled out a canvas bag. A cat was screaming and thrashing inside it.

Oren took the bag to the window as Bernheim and McGruder got to their feet.

"If you make one step toward me," Oren said, "I'm throwing the cat out the window."

"Don't be a fool," McGruder said. "Give us the cat and we'll see that the police go easy on you."

"Give them the cat," Carl yelled to Oren.

"You want the cat?" Oren shouted hysterically. "Go get him." He threw the canvas bag out of the second-story window and it landed with a thud.

"Oh, my God," McGruder cried as he dashed down the steps. He rushed over to the canvas bag. The cat was still screaming and thrashing inside. He opened up the bag gently, talking in a soothing voice. "It's all right, Irving. It's all right."

Slowly the cat calmed down. First his head peered out of the bag. McGruder took the cat in his arms and petted him gently. "Don't worry, Irving. You won't be hurt anymore."

McGruder heard struggling and furniture breaking in the apartment.

He looked up at the window. Suddenly Bernheim's face appeared. "Is Irving all right?"

"Yes. Are you?"

"Just fine. Americans do not know that the French fight with their feet. We better call the police."

But Maria had already done it. A police car with sirens wailing came up the driveway. Out stepped two uniformed men, their pistols drawn.

"What's going on?" one of the policemen asked.

McGruder, still holding the cat, said, "There are a couple of cat killers up there in the apartment."

"What did you say?"

"Do you know about Irving?" McGruder asked.

"You mean the one that does all those terrific commercials on television?" the policeman said. "My kid loves that cat."

"The men up there kidnapped him and were holding him for a hundred-thousand-dollar ransom. When we found their hideout they threw Irving out the window."

"What a bunch of filthy crumbs," the policeman said.

They rushed upstairs to the apartment and three minutes later they came downstairs with Oren and Carl in handcuffs.

"Let's all go to the main house and get your statements," the policeman said.

McGruder went first, followed by Inspector Bernheim, the two handcuffed men, and the police. Maria and the housekeeper were waiting by the door.

Maria screamed with joy when she saw McGruder holding the cat.

"You found Irving."

They all went into the living room. The cat

was very nervous and tried to jump out of McGruder's arms.

"What's that all over your suit?" Maria asked.

Inspector Bernheim went over to McGruder. "It looks like paint—white paint."

McGruder looked down at his hands. They also were covered with white paint. "Oh, my gosh," McGruder said. "The cat's been painted."

Maria looked at the animal closely. "That isn't Irving."

"Are you sure?" Bernheim asked.

McGruder stared at the cat in shock. "No, it isn't Irving."

Oren chuckled. "We don't have Irving. We were going to give you this dumb cat in his place. We painted him to look like Irving."

Carl said, "It was his idea. I had nothing to do with it."

"Where is Irving?" Inspector Bernheim said.

"I have no clue," Oren said. "I picked him up from my aunt's place and I was going to hide him in my apartment in the Village because I knew he was worth something to the Pussyfoot Cat Food Company. I figured the old lady would kick the bucket and then you'd have to deal with me. But then I read all the stories in the newspapers and I decided you were desperate and I got the ransom gimmick. I locked Irving in my bathroom and went out to buy some rope for him. But I forgot I had left the window open, and when I returned, Irving was gone. At first I thought I was a dead duck, but I figured if I didn't know where Irving was, neither did you. So I caught another cat, put him in a bag, and came out here to see Carl. The cemetery was Carl's idea."

"But he wanted to kill the cat," Carl said.

"I didn't want to kill any cat," said Oren coldly. "I wanted to kill Irving. You don't know what it's like to see a cat on television night and day and know he's making more money than you are. My aunt loved that cat more than she loved me. She's always loved cats more than she's loved me. Well, I decided I was going to fix my aunt once and for all."

"How did you know Miss Summersby was sick?" Inspector Bernheim asked him.

"She called me that morning and said she was going to the hospital. She wanted me to take Irving to the Pussyfoot Cat Food Company so he could do his commercial. But I had no intention of letting him do another commercial. I was going to take that rope I bought and . . ."

"Stop," cried Maria.

"Lock them up," said McGruder in disgust.

"What's the charge?" Oren demanded.

The policeman whose daughter loved Irving said, "Embezzlement, catnapping, intent to murder, and depriving a domestic animal of its civil rights. With a jury of cat lovers, you both could get life."

The two policemen pushed Oren and Carl out the front door.

McGruder had placed the frightened cat down on the rug and he jumped up on the sofa.

"My sofa," the housekeeper screamed. "He's getting white paint all over my sofa." The cat then jumped into a beautiful silk chair. More white paint on the furniture. The housekeeper started to chase the cat all over the house.

McGruder, his suit covered with paint, sank into a chair. The other two sat down as well. They were all exhausted.

"What do we do now?" McGruder asked.

"I guess we'd better get some sleep," Inspector Bernheim said.

"Good-bye, Super Bowl," McGruder said.

"Good-bye, Irving," Maria added.

They drove back to New York in silence.

Once McGruder mumbled, "Where on earth could that stupid cat be?"

Inspector Bernheim sat up in his seat. "Wait, I have just thought of something. Remember I told you when we drove out that in France a cat knows when his mistress is dying and will not move from her bed. Suppose Irving knows Miss Summersby's dying. Where would he be?"

"At the hospital?" Maria said.

"No," said Bernheim. "He doesn't know where the hospital is."

McGruder said, "On Miss Summersby's bed?"

"But we were there and the cat was gone," Maria protested.

"You were there two days ago," Bernheim said.

"Drive to Miss Summersby's house," Bernheim ordered McGruder.

They arrived just as dawn was breaking over New York. They rang the bell. It took fifteen minutes for the lady to answer it. It was the same woman Maria and McGruder had spoken to on the first day.

"Is Irving back?" McGruder asked.

"Of course, she's back," the woman said.

"She?" Maria said.

"Naturally, Irving's a she. She's going to have kittens."

McGruder couldn't believe his ears.

"Why would Miss Summersby name a female cat Irving?"

"Because," said the woman huffily, "her father's name was Irving and she always named her cats after him."

"Can we go up and see her?" Bernheim asked.

"Miss Summersby said it was all right. We need her for a commercial," McGruder said.

"I don't know if I should give Irving to you without Miss Summersby's permission."

McGruder cried, "But we have to do this commercial."

"No skin off my back," the woman said.

Inspector Bernheim took fifty dollars out of his pocket.

"Miss Summersby asked us to give this to you to pay her next month's rent."

The woman looked at the money. "Well, in that case take her. But bring her back when you're done with her. Miss Summersby lives on the third floor in the back."

The three rushed upstairs and opened the door to Miss Summersby's neat apartment. There was Irving sitting on the bed as if in mourning. Her sad eyes looked up at the people and then she looked at the empty pillow.

Maria lifted her gently in her arms. "You poor darling. No one told us you were a woman."

McGruder said, "Come on. We don't have much time. We have to get him—her—down to the studio. If we're lucky, we can get the commercial done in time."

As they were leaving, the landlady stood there, her arms folded. "Why didn't you tell us Irving had come back?" McGruder said.

"How did I know you were interested?" the landlady snorted.

"But didn't you read in the papers about the search?"

"I don't have time to read the papers," the woman said. "And bring that cat back."

As soon as word got around the Pussyfoot Cat

Food Company that Irving was back, everyone rushed for the studio. Mr. and Mrs. Pettibone dashed in. So did several newspapermen who had waited all night to get any fresh news of Irving's disappearance.

McGruder had his coat off, the one with all the paint on it, and was shouting orders in his shirt-sleeves. "Put the can there," he said to a stage-hand. Then to the cameraman, "I want a tight shot first of the can—make sure we see the words Chicken Salad on the Pussyfoot label. Then a close-up of Irving's face. Then pull back and just shoot as Irving eats the chicken salad with her paw. Fix those lights. Now, everyone in the studio quiet—we're going for a take. Are we all ready? Maria, put Irving next to the can."

Maria, who was holding Irving close to her bosom, placed the cat gently next to the can of chicken salad.

"ACTION" McGruder yelled.

"There's something wrong with the camera," the TV cameraman cried.

"Holy smoke," said Mr. McGruder. "I forgot I put the ransom money in the camera."

The cameraman opened up the back of his camera and a thousand $100 bills fell out.

Everyone in the studio was gogglyeyed.

"My money," Mr. Pettibone cried.

"Forget the money," said McGruder. "Let's get the commercial done."

The cameraman left the money on the floor and started focusing on Irving. "ACTION," McGruder shouted again.

Irving just sat there.

"She's not eating it," Zelda Pettibone cried.

"Eat the damn food, Irving, or I'll throttle you," Mr. Pettibone shouted.

"Cut!" said McGruder. "Maybe she doesn't like chicken salad."

"Then give her the tuna fish in the chicken salad can," Pettibone said. "Who will know the difference?"

One of McGruder's assistants emptied out the chicken salad and replaced it with tuna fish. He placed it in front of Irving. She wouldn't touch it.

"Irving," screamed McGruder between burps, "do you know what I've gone through for you? Please stick your dumb paw in the can and start eating."

Irving looked around at all the people and just blinked.

"Wait a minute," said Maria. "I have an idea. The landlady said Irving was pregnant. Why don't you put some pickles in with the cat food?"

"Pickles?" McGruder said.

"Well, women like pickles when they're pregnant. Maybe cats do too."

McGruder said, "We have nothing to lose. Get some pickles," he yelled at his assistant.

"Dill or sweet?" the assistant asked.

"Dill," said Maria.

"Pickles in cat food?" Zelda Pettibone moaned. "I've never heard of anything so outrageous."

McGruder gathered up all the money while they were waiting and threw it into a box.

Inspector Bernheim said, "I've never seen them make a television commercial before. This is very interesting."

The assistant was back in ten minutes. He dumped pieces of dill pickle into the can. Before the cameras could even start rolling. Irving began to eat from the can with her paw.

"She likes it," yelled Mr. Pettibone.

"She's eating it," cried Mrs. Pettibone.

"Okay, let's go for a take," McGruder said.

Just as the camera zeroed in on the can, a secretary rushed in and said, "Mr. McGruder, there is a very important telephone call for you."

"I'm busy," McGruder screamed.

"It's a Doctor Parker at St. Luke's Hospital. He says he has to talk to you."

"CUT" screamed McGruder. He went over to the wall and grabbed the phone. "What is it?"

"This is Doctor Parker. Miss Summersby is fading fast. She keeps asking for Irving."

"Tell her she's okay," McGruder said. "Tell her we'll bring her over as soon as we finish the commercial."

"It may be too late then. She won't belive Irving is all right. If you don't get the cat over here within the hour, Miss Summersby will be dead."

McGruder hung up the phone slowly.

"Can we get on with the commercial?" Pettibone demanded.

"There isn't going to be any commercial. We've got to get Irving over to St. Luke's Hospital," McGruder said wearily.

"Are you crazy?" The network won't take it if we don't get our commercial over there by noon."

I don't have to time to explain," McGruder said, "but a life is at stake."

"Your life is at stake," Pettibone shouted. "You're finished, McGruder. "You'll never work in advertising again."

"Maria," said McGruder, "grab Irving. We don't have much time."

Maria picked up Irving and dashed out with McGruder, who was in his shirtsleeves. Bernheim was right behind them. They stopped the first cab that came by and McGruder said to the driver, "St. Luke's Hospital and step on it—it's a matter of life and death!"

Sunday, millions of people all over America were sitting in front of their seats watching the Super Bowl. Part of this audience were four people in Room 304 at St. Luke's Hospital. Miss Summersby was propped up in her bed, having made a miraculous recovery. Sitting in three chairs in the room were McGruder, Maria, and Inspector Alain Pierre Bernheim.

At Miss Summersby's feet was Irving, holding a pickle in her paw and gnawing on it.

The announcer on television said, "And now let's pause for a commercial." On the screen came a cat. A voice said, "Simon, what do you think of Pussyfoot's new Chicken Salad Cat Food?" The cat did a somersault in the air. "Don't you want every cat to eat Pussyfoot Chicken Salad?" The cat did another somersault in the air. The voice said, "If Simon flips for Pussyfoot, just watch and see what your cat docs."

McGruder said, "It stinks."

"It's awful," said Maria.

"I would never let Irving do anything that commercial," Miss Summersby agreed.

The Super Bowl was a big success for everyone except the Pussyfoot Cat Food Company. Sales of all Pussyfoot cans started to plummet. In two months Pussyfoot was almost bankrupt. But McGruder and Maria couldn't have cared less. They had gotten married and were honeymooning in Hawaii. It was there that Mr. Pettibone traced them and begged McGruder to come back and work for him. McGruder refused. Then Zelda Pettibone came on the phone and said that if McGruder came back he could become president of Pussyfoot.

It was a very tempting offer, particularly since Irving had given birth to five kittens and all of them ate cat food with their paws.

He told Zelda Pettibone he would come back on the following conditions. Irving and her kittens would receive $1,500 a week, which would be paid to Miss Summersby. The Pussyfoot Company would build a cat hospital in New York that would give free medical care to any cat who was ill. And, finally, the name of all future Pussyfoot Cat Food would be called Irving's Delight.

Mrs. Pettibone agreed to all the terms.

The rest is history. Irving's Delight is now the most popular cat food in America and its Chicken Salad was given a gold medal at the Tokyo World's Fair.

As for Inspector Alain Pierre Bernheim, he is now working for the British Government in Scotland trying to find the Loch Ness Monster. In the evenings he sits around the pub with the people from the area and tells them about his most interesting case. "It had to do," he says, "with this strange cat who would only eat cat food from a can with her paw ..."

the Relaxation Response

by Herbert Benson, M.D.

with Miriam Z. Klipper

Nationwide
#1
Bestseller

It could be the most important book of your life!

A simple meditative technique that has helped millions to cope with fatigue, anxiety and stress. Featured in *Family Circle, House and Garden, Good Housekeeping* and scores of magazines and newspapers across the country.

"In transcendental meditation you pay $125 and you get your mantra. You may do as well by reading *The Relaxation Response*."

Money

AVON   29439/$1.95   TRR 8-76

THE BIG BESTSELLERS
ARE AVON BOOKS

THE END OF AN EMPIRE . . .
THE BURNING HOPES OF TEEMING MASSES . . .
THE BLAZING DAWN OF A NEW NATION!

THE THUNDERING INTERNATIONAL BESTSELLER

FREEDOM AT MIDNIGHT

LARRY COLLINS/DOMINIQUE LAPIERRE
authors of IS PARIS BURNING?

In a story of epic scope and sweeping grandeur, the bestselling Collins and Lapierre recreate the endless bloodbaths, the frenzied riots and the brutal assassinations that climaxed with the end of British rule in India.

The raging tumult of an era comes alive in the towering figures of Mountbatten, Nehru, Churchill and Gandhi, as FREEDOM AT MIDNIGHT unfolds against the world's most exotic backdrop.

"The song of India . . . illuminated like scenes in a pageant."
TIME

29587/$2.25
With 32 pages of photographs